KITTY QUEST
TRIAL BY TENTACLE

WRITTEN & ILLUSTRATED
BY PHIL CORBETT

SIMON & SCHUS

First published in Great Britain in 2022 by Simon & Schuster UK Ltd

First published in the USA in 2022 by Razorbill,
an imprint of Penguin Random House LLC, New York

Text and illustrations copyright © 2022 Phil Corbett

1 3 5 7 9 10 8 6 4 2

Simon & Schuster UK Ltd
1st Floor, 222 Gray's Inn Road
London
WC1X 8HB

www.simonandschuster.co.uk
www.simonandschuster.com.au
www.simonandschuster.co.in

Simon & Schuster Australia, Sydney
Simon & Schuster India, New Delhi

A CIP catalogue record for this book is available from the British Library.

PB ISBN 978-1-3985-0472-1
eBook ISBN 978-1-3985-0473-8

Printed in China
Design by Maria Fazio

MIX
Paper from
responsible sources
FSC® C020471

SHROOMING SEASON IS THE BEST. MY BASKET IS FULL ALREADY. HOW ARE YOU DOING, WOOLFRIK?

MY MUM SAYS THAT WHEN IT COMES TO FUNGI...

IT'S BEST TO GO BIG.

OH.

AAAARRGGHHHHHHHHH!

THIS IS SUCH A RELAXING WAY TO SPEND A MORNING.

PERIGOLD! DO SOMETHING!

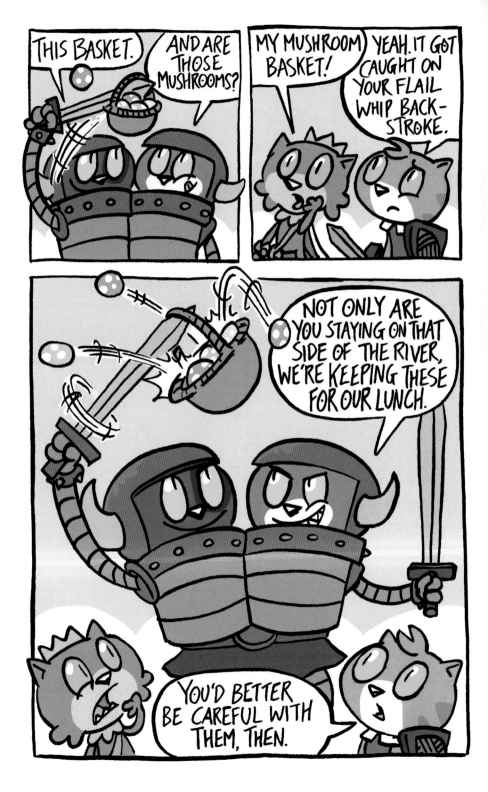

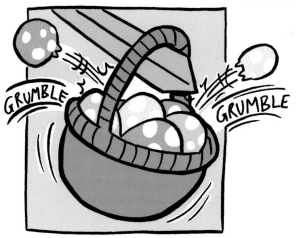

DOES THIS COUNT AS A WIN?

I SAY WE TAKE IT.

INDEED, IT IS YOUR VICTORY.

WE HAVE FALLEN. WE BOW TO YOU.

AS THE VICTORS, WHAT ARE YOUR DEMANDS OF US?

WE JUST WANT YOU TO LET PEOPLE USE THIS BRIDGE. THAT'S ALL.

BOW

HANG ON, WOOLFRIK, THEY WANT SOME DEMANDS.

IT WOULD BE RUDE NOT TO GIVE THEM ANY.

THIS IS A REALLY GOOD SWORD.

THERE'S MORE IN HERE, TOO.

IT'S A BOOKLET ON BRIDGE GUARDING.

BRIDGE GUARDING? WHAT'S THAT?

WELL, ACORDING TO THIS, YOU LITERALLY CLAIM A BRIDGE...

AND GUARD IT.

GUARD IT? FROM WHAT?

EVERYTHING, I SUPPOSE.

AND THIS RUSTY PILE OF METAL IS GUARDIAN ARMOUR. HOP IN. LET'S TRY IT OUT.

I DON'T SEE WHY NOT. WHAT DO YOU THINK, PERIGOLD?

HUH?

SORRY. WHAT DID YOU SAY? I WASN'T LISTENING. I WAS RUMMAGING THROUGH THIS BATTLE SUIT.

I SAID THAT AS LONG AS THEY LET PEOPLE CROSS, THEY COULD STILL GUARD THE BRIDGE.

AND TO BE CLEAR, THAT'S LETTING THEM CROSS WITH NO FIGHTING?

DEFINITELY NO FIGHTING.

I FOUND THE BRIDGE-GUARDING BOOKLET IN YOUR ARMOUR.

BRIDGE GUARDING

THERE'S QUITE A LOT IN HERE ON GUARDING A BRIDGE WITHOUT RESORTING TO FIGHTS.

WE SHOULD GO MUSHROOM HUNTING MORE OFTEN.
FUN AS IT IS, I FIND THE COUNTRYSIDE TO BE TOO WEIRD. I MUCH PREFER CITY LIFE, WHERE EVERYTHING IS NORMAL.
MEOWMINSTER

I AGREE. I LOVE MUSHROOMS...

I'M WORRIED ABOUT THIS SAUCE.

...BUT MORTIMORE IS NO CHEF.

HE'S GOING TO RUIN ALL THESE MUSHROOMS THAT WE GATHERED.

AND THAT BLUE ONE ALMOST KILLED YOU, TOO.

I WOULDN'T SAY THAT. I WAS NEVER IN ANY REAL DANGER.

THAT GHOST CAN'T EVEN TASTE HIS OWN COOKING. IT'S US WHO SUFFER, EATING IT.

WE'RE HERE AND ≡GASP≡ WHAT'S THAT STENCH?

MORTIMORE LOVES POTTERING AROUND IN THE KITQUAROO KITCHEN.

AND HE LOVES COOKING, SO BE NICE. AFTER YOU.

MORTIMORE, SLOW DOWN. I STILL GET LOST IN HERE. IT'S MASSIVE.

WE CAN'T ALL WALK THROUGH WALLS, YOU KNOW.

ALSO, I DON'T THINK THAT THE TOWER OF KITQUAROO IS AN ACCURATE NAME FOR THIS PLACE, SEEING AS SO MUCH OF IT IS UNDERGROUND.

THE TOWER IS THE IMPORTANT PART. IT'S INSPIRATIONAL.

THE DUNGEONS OF KITQUAROO WOULD GIVE THE WRONG IMPRESSION.

OH, THEY ARE. GRASPURTS ARE FEROCIOUS MONSTERS THAT USUALLY LIVE DEEP BELOW THE SEA.

BUT THE REQUESTS BOX IS FULL OF LOCAL SIGHTINGS.

REQUESTS

WHICH ISN'T GOOD AT ALL. A GRASPURT ON LAND IS BAD NEWS.

MAYBE THEY'RE HERE FOR SOMETHING NICE AND INNOCENT.

DO THEY LIKE MUSIC? MAYBE THEY'RE HERE FOR THE YARN FESTIVAL.

OH YES. I LOVE YARNFEST!

LAST YEAR'S WAS AMAZING. I REMEMBER YOU GETTING THAT COMMEMORATIVE SHIRT.

FEST

THERE ARE REPORTS OF THEM BEING ACCOMPLISHED MUSICIANS. LOOK AT THIS.

WHAT KIND OF INSTRUMENT IS THAT?

IT'S CALLED A SLAUGHTER HORN. THEY TRADITIONALLY PLAY THEM BEFORE THEIR ARMIES ATTACK.

I CAN'T SEE THAT GOING DOWN WELL AT YARNFEST.

I DON'T KNOW. YARNFEST CROWDS CAN BE PRETTY ROWDY.

OH MY GOODNIGHT! YOU ARE SCARY!

I BEG YOUR PARDON.

ER... NOTHING. WE'RE JUST TWO ORDINARY BEACHGOERS ENJOYING THIS ORDINARY, RUN-OF-THE-MILL BEACH.

DOING ORDINARY BEACH ACTIVITIES LIKE EATING DELICIOUS ICE CREAM.

YUM.

THOSE AREN'T ICE CREAMS. THEY'RE CLEARLY HERMIT CRABS. I JUST SAW YOU PICK THEM UP.

OUCH! MINE NIPPED ME!

THOSE THINGS LOOK DANGEROUS, UGLY, AND REALLY SCARY. WHAT SHOULD WE DO?
I SUPPOSE JUST WHAT MORTIMORE ADVISED. STAY HIDDEN AND SPY ON THEM FOR INFORMATION.
AND YOU CAN LEAVE ME OUT OF IT, TOO.
GOOD LUCK!

BUT FORGIVE ME. WHERE ARE MY MANNERS?

CAPTAIN BUBBLES, RELEASE THEM.

DROP

YOU LUCKY PAIR ARE IN THE PRESENCE OF MARINE ROYALTY. YOU CAN TELL THAT FROM MY EXOTIC FRILLS.

SWOOSH!

LOOK AT IT, THOUGH! WITH THE SUNFLOWERS IN IT, I THOUGHT THAT HORRIBLE TWO-HEADED MONSTER WAS BACK.

NO OFFENCE.

NONE TAKEN.

HMM. THIS GIVES ME AN IDEA.

IF THIS SUIT OF ARMOUR TERRIFIED YOU, WOOLFRIK.

I WOULDN'T SAY "TERRIFIED". IT WAS JUST A BIT OF A SHOCK, THAT'S ALL.

THAT'S SETTLED, THEN. WOOLFRIK, ARE YOU THINKING WHAT I'M THINKING?

THAT WE USE IT TO SPEED THROUGH THE FOREST TO MAKE UP FOR THE TIME WE WASTED EATING THESE LOVELY DROP SCONES AND DRINKING THIS DELIGHTFUL DANDELION AND BURDOCK SODA WHEN WE SHOULD HAVE BEEN RACING TOWARD MEOWMINSTER TO WARN THEM ABOUT THE IMMINENT GRASPURT INVASION?

AND PERIGOLD, WE'VE TALKED ABOUT STANDING ON TABLES.

OF COURSE NOT. WE'RE GETTING IN THAT SUIT AND WE'RE GOING TO FIGHT THOSE GRASPURTS OURSELVES!

THAT WILL NEVER FOOL THEM.

GRASPURTS DON'T DO DETAILS. THEY'RE SEA CREATURES. THEY HAVE TERRIBLE EYESIGHT ON LAND.

THEY SAID SO THEMSELVES.

HMM. TRUE. THEY DID SAY THAT.

CLEVERLY DISGUISED IN THE SUIT, WE'LL BE OUR OWN GRASPURT CHAMPION!

IT'S THE PERFECT PLOY: STEALTH AND CUNNING, LIKE MORTIMORE SAID.

RIGHT. GOODBYE, FLOWERS.

"NO WAY" WHAT?

NO WAY WILL YOU MANAGE TO PILOT IT.

CAN YOU TEACH US?

MAYBE. HOW LONG HAVE YOU GOT?

AN HOUR.

ALTHOUGH IT TOOK US TEN MINUTES TO GET HERE, SO ANOTHER TEN TO GET BACK, THEN FIVE MORE MINUTES TO GET BACK TO THE BEACH.

THEN WE SPENT FIVE MINUTES DRINKING YOUR LOVELY SODA AND EATING YOUR DELICIOUS SCONES.

SO HALF AN HOUR, THEN.

I RECKON THAT'S DOABLE.

NOW THAT YOU'VE MASTERED WALKING...

"MASTERED"?

NOW THAT YOU KNOW THE BASICS OF WALKING, LET'S GIVES THE ARMS A GO.

SEE IF YOU CAN BEND DOWN AND PICK UP YOUR TRIDENT.

I FEEL CONFIDENT THAT WE CAN.

IMAGINE THAT THE ARMOUR'S ARMS ARE YOURS, JUST LONGER AND MUCH, MUCH STRONGER.

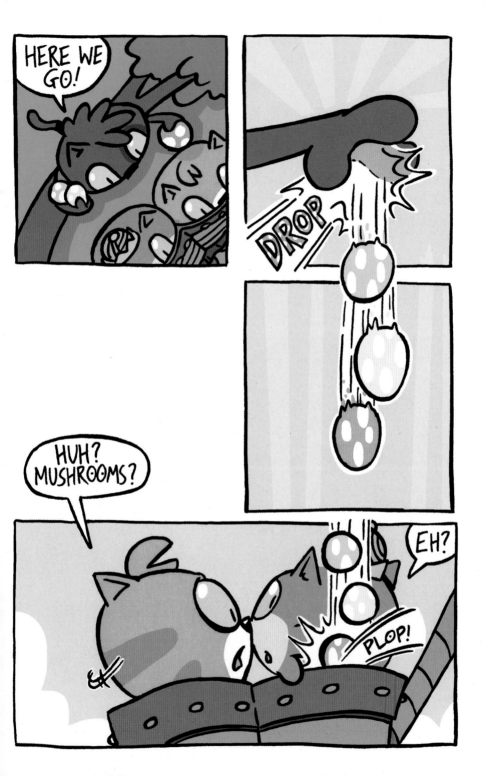

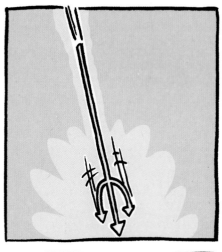

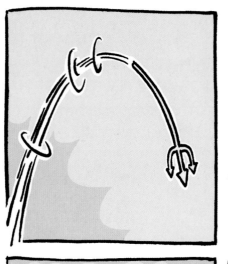

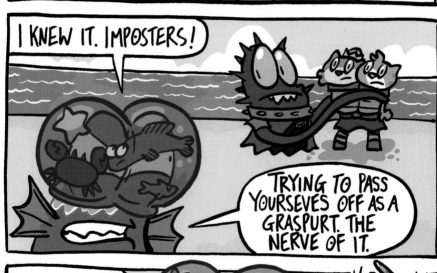

WE HAVE TO SAVE MEOWMINSTER.

YOU NO GO ANYWHERE.

ARE YOU SURE ABOUT THAT? PERIGOLD?